Acclaim for *Little Garlic*

"Happily, Avideh Shashaani brings us 'Little Garlic' who I believe lives in every one's heart, especially children— and who gives us back the magic of a world unruined."

GRACE CAVALIERI
Maryland Poet Laureate

"The world—through your witness—has nothing to lose and everything to gain."

RICHARD ROHR
Founder, THE CENTER FOR ACTION AND CONTEMPLATION;
Internationally Recognized Author and Spiritual Leader

"Avideh Shashaani has written a family story that surpasses the standard of a myth. Here, welcome into a timeless spiritual parable, as old as the protagonist, 'Little Garlic,' who faces steep challenges to then discover deeper realities, all through a process of peeling back layers of truth by the guide, 'Onion,' the Virgil of our story."

LISA MILLER, Ph.D.
Professor of Psychology and Education, Teachers College, Columbia
University; Author, *The Awakened Brain* and the *New York Times*
Bestseller, *The Spiritual Child: The New Science of Parenting for Health
and Lifelong Thriving*

"A spiritual bridge between the young and old. The book reminds us that true words of spiritual wisdom appeal to all ages."

ROB LEHMAN
Trustee, FETZER INSTITUTE

Little Garlic

Enchanted Tales for All Ages

Avideh Shashaani

Wyatt-MacKenzie Publishing
DEADWOOD, OREGON

Little Garlic: Enchanted Tales for All Ages
Avideh Shashaani

F I R S T   E D I T I O N

Hardcover ISBN: 978-1-954332-00-3
Softcover ISBN: 978-1-954332-01-0
eBook ISBN: 978-1-954332-02-7

Library of Congress Control Number: 2021932152

Wyatt-MacKenzie Publishing
D E A D W O O D ,   O R E G O N

For further information contact: info@wyattmackenzie.com

Dedicated to all children of the world, especially those who need a friend.

Contents

Introduction

NOT SINCE MISTER ROGERS have we had a work for children that is so purely true, without manipulation and sensationalism. The authentic and the unadorned come together here in a lonely creature's quest. We are back to simplicity of knowing what a child is, and how that child can be enchanted by elegant imagination.

What children read, children will believe. This book was written so that the young would once again believe in a loving world, one that exists even now beneath our daily surface; a story brought to light with the adventures of Little Garlic.

Little Garlic is born, alone, and alienated. However, the kindness of others brings him to understanding about what the world contains, and how he can be nourished by guided experiences.

Children's literature has taken us into every passage of human conduct but seems to have lost the essence of our original intent for children—bringing them from innocence to growth, and then to loving impressions of a fulfilled life.

In simple language, and clear action, this book will take us once more into the lost lands of fairytale, folklore, and the magic existence of creatures working for the good.

Grace Cavalieri
Maryland Poet Laureate

Foreword

AVIDEH SHASHAANI HAS WRITTEN a family story
that surpasses the standard of a myth. Here,
welcome into a timeless spiritual parable, as old as the
protagonist, "Little Garlic," who faces steep challenges
to then discover deeper realities, all through a process
of peeling back layers of truth by the guide, "Onion,"
the Virgil of our story.

Shashaani speaks to the child as a wise knower.
She engages the child's deep birthright, of inborn
spiritual awareness. Crossing between layers of human
reality, this story book has the potency to be a foundational story in a child's life.

Shashaani joins with the natural wisdom of the
child, through the eyes of the protagonist. A journeying

Little Garlic naturally sees all living beings as alive and conscious, and so can learn from all beings. Throughout the encounters of the quest, the author accurately honors the child's capability of knowing and engaging multiple layers of consciousness; the dream world, the companionship and friendship in nature, in a cow or flower, and a timeless spirit or truth.

In offering our children a spiritually grounded journey, Shashaani's book will strengthen the child's natural ability to hear, feel, and love the vital surrounding world. She speaks to this place of knowing, the seat of awareness through which the physical order of reality reveals the foundational spiritual reality, where the child finds an enduring home. A centered place to live joyfully, beautifully with companionship, as The Flower, with hope and peace. Here at home in the universe, the child carries true resilience from loss and suffering, even renewal in the face of devastation of family and community or origin, with the felt knowing of being held and loved by life itself.

If a parent reads from this lyrical book several times a week to the young child, who then returns to these vital passages when of reading age, and who should then reach for these well-loved stories as an autonomous middle-school child, it is most likely that for the rest of her or his life, the child will feel the embrace of the goodness in the world, and the door will remain open to the inner passageway to spiritual discovery. And the child's family will be transformed back to its Edenic nature.

Lisa Miller, Ph.D.
Author of *The Awakened Brain: The New Science of Spirituality and Our Quest for an Inspired Life* and *The Spiritual Child: The New Science of Parenting for Health and Lifelong Thriving*; Professor of Psychology and Education, Founding Director, THE SPIRITUALITY AND MIND BODY INSTITUTE, Teachers College, Columbia Univ.

The Special Meeting

ONCE UPON A TIME—anywhere from a thousand years to a year ago—and somewhere not too far from us and not too near to us, Little Garlic sat all by himself, forlorn and sad. Little tears dropped gently from his lonely eyes and fell to the ground where slender green leaves had grown all around him, protecting him from the sand and wind that blew his way.

One day, an onion was blown by the wind and landed close to our Little Garlic. Onion looked around and saw Little Garlic sitting all by himself. He said, "Hey little fella, what's your name, and why are you so sad?"

Little Garlic, who had been by himself for such a long time, couldn't contain himself, and his tears began to swell up and flow like an endless river all around him. He lifted his eyes and looked at Onion, sighed a deep sigh, and said, "My story will make you very sad."

"Don't worry, little fella," Onion answered. "I'm here for you. Why don't you start from the very beginning and tell me your story."

Little Garlic began to share with Onion his sad tale. He said, "One day, when I was barely above the ground, a wild wind plucked me out and blew me away from my land and home and brought me here. I don't know where I came from. I don't know who I am. I don't have a name. I don't know what I look like. All I know is that everyone calls me 'Stinky' and no one wants to be around me!"

Onion said, "Not to worry, little fella, we have a lot of time to figure it all out!

"Let me introduce myself. My name is Onion and I believe you are from the garlic family. Is it okay if sometimes I call you, 'Little Garlic'?"

"Of course, it's okay!" Little Garlic was very happy that he had finally met someone who knew something about his family and said, "I'm so happy to meet you.

Is it okay if I tell you what's happened to me ever since the wind brought me here?"

Onion, in a reassuring and kind voice, said, "Of course, I want to hear everything."

Little Garlic finally felt that someone really cared for him. So, he told Onion everything that had happened to him ever since the wind had brought him to this strange place away from his home and family. Onion listened very carefully to every word of Little Garlic's sad story.

"Stinky, my foot!" exclaimed Onion. "Do you have any idea how your ancestors survived and spread out to so many countries and conquered the hearts of so many people all over the world?

"Those people who called you 'Stinky' didn't know any better. They didn't know anything about your history, culture, or geography.

"Just show me how many of them would be able to survive if they traveled through the roughest and most dangerous mountains, and how many of them are beloved by so many people of different races and cultures.

5

"Stinky my foot! They should figure out how to conquer hearts and not pick on little ones like you."

Little Garlic was listening very carefully to what Onion was saying but looked a little puzzled. He didn't understand what it meant to conquer hearts and he didn't know anything about ancestors.

Noticing Little Garlic's confusion, Onion said, "All right, let me give it to you straight. Even better, we'll go on a journey together so you can find out all the answers for yourself, but there's one thing you must first do."

"Onion, what is it that I must first do? I'm scared. I don't know how to go on a journey. I'm so tiny. I don't know anything."

Onion said, "Sometimes it's better to learn for yourself, but I will help you. We can figure it out together."

"Okay, Onion. Do you think I can do it?"

"Of course, I have no doubt, little fella. Listen very carefully to what I'm going to share with you now.

"You don't know this yet, but everything has a special secret that is kept in a very secret place and it's hidden from all eyes. It's a treasure that you must discover for yourself."

"Onion, I'm scared. I don't know anything about secrets. It sounds too difficult. I'm so tiny."

Onion in a reassuring and kind voice said, "Come here, little fella, and sit right next to me. I want to tell you a story that will help you understand.

"Just like you, when I was really tiny, the wind blew me away from my home, family, and everything around me. I landed in a place where I didn't know anyone. I cried and cried. I was so lonesome and scared. I had no one.

"One day, a little boy was walking along and just happened to sit by me. He looked sad and alone. I asked him why he was so sad.

"He began to tell me his story while tears poured from his eyes. He said every day when he'd go to school, the kids would pick on him. They'd make fun of him and call him all kinds of names. No one played with him and they pushed him around and told him he was different.

"So, I asked him if he had a family and if they

could help him. He said he did have a family, but they didn't know what was going on in school. He said that each day after school, before going home, he'd go for a walk and find a quiet place to sit by himself and cry, so he wouldn't take his sadness home with him.

"I asked him why he didn't tell his family about his troubles in school. He said that his parents loved him very much and he didn't want to get them upset.

"I told him that if I had a family who loved me, I would tell them what's going on, and they would be able to help. My friend said that it sounded like a good idea and he would tell them.

"Then he asked me why I was so sad and all by myself. I slowly told him my story and we began to cry together.

"Then, he said, 'Why don't we become friends! I'll take you home with me, and you can stay with me and we'll be best friends.'

"Well, this sounded like a miracle. How could this wonderful thing happen to me—a tiny little Onion!"

By now, several hours had passed since Onion had begun to share his story with Little Garlic. Onion noticed that the sun had set. It was dusk, and Onion looked up and saw the very first stars in the sky.

In a whisper, Onion continued to share his friendship with the little boy. When he had finished his story, Little Garlic said, "Our stories are so much alike, but how come you're not sad like me? What happened to make you so carefree and cheerful?"

"You see, little fella, it only took one person—that little boy—to see who I really was. His friendship changed everything for me.

"You see, I have many, many layers, and it was difficult for people to see through all these layers. So they judged me by what I looked like and they called me 'Stinky'—just like you. I always blamed others for not wanting to be around me. Now that I've gotten to know myself, I understand others much better."

Little Garlic was so relaxed that he gave a big yawn. Onion, realizing that it was getting late, said, "We can talk about this tomorrow. Let's get a good night's rest and wake up in the morning to a brand-new day! We have a long journey ahead.

"Now, close your eyes, relax, and let the gentle

breeze of the night and the light of the stars fill you up with a feeling of peace and happiness.

"Good night little fella. Sweet dreams."

"Good night, Onion. Thank you for being my friend."

Little Garlic closed his eyes with a feeling of comfort. For the very first time since the wind had brought him to this place, he was able to go to sleep without a care in the world. He slept deeply, feeling grateful that he had found a friend.

By now, the entire sky was filled with stars, and a blanket of calm had settled across the night sky.

Onion gazed at the star-filled sky and remembered how he had been guided and how he had found his own secret along the mysterious path of life.

Onion glanced over and saw that Little Garlic was happily asleep. He, too, closed his eyes with a feeling of gratitude for having found a new friend.

The Ancestors

I T WAS NEARLY DAYBREAK when Onion opened his eyes and saw Little Garlic, deeply asleep. He looked at his little friend with the tender eyes of a loving mother and began to think of the long journey ahead.

The sun was casting its glow across the horizon and the birds were chirping away, already busy with their daily activities.

Little Garlic began to stir, then slowly opened his eyes to a brand-new day.

"Good morning, little fella!"

"Good morning, Onion!"

"Are you ready to start the day?" Onion asked.

"I slept so well and had so many wonderful dreams that I'm ready for anything."

Onion smiled. "That's good to hear. Are you ready to hear some special secrets?"

"Wow, that sounds exciting! But what are secrets?"

"Do you remember how yesterday you told me that people call you 'Stinky' and no one wanted to be around you? And I said that they just didn't know any better?"

Little Garlic said, "Yes, I remember."

"Well then, let's start from the very beginning. Just by looking at you, I can tell that you've come a very long way from your homeland."

"How can you tell?" Little Garlic asked.

"Your appearance tells me that your origins—that is, your very, very beginnings—are in the mountains in a very distant place. As to why you're here, I know for sure that you were brought here for a purpose. We all have a reason for being where we are, and it's a magical experience when we find out."

Little Garlic was getting confused. He couldn't understand what Onion was talking about.

Seeing the confusion on Little Garlic's face, Onion said, "You'll figure it all out as we go on the journey.

16

But first, let me tell you a little story about the magic that surrounds your ancestors."

Little Garlic got even more confused and asked, "What's magic and what are ancestors?"

"Just be patient, little fella. I'm going to share a few stories with you, and you'll understand.

"You and I are actually related, but you have a very important ancestry. Your ancestors, meaning all the family members who came before you, were present at the beginning of time.

"Those who call you 'Stinky' don't know who you are and don't know your true value. If they did, they wouldn't leave you alone.

"Why, who knows what would've happened to you if they did! Sometimes being underestimated is a gift, and you're very lucky."

Onion went on to tell Little Garlic the story of how humans had learned to use the many gifts from nature to their advantage for health, healing, and a long life. He also explained how humans can sometimes be too greedy and take too much without giving back.

17

Little Garlic kept thinking how ignorant he'd been and how he had no clue about anything at all! He learned that humans in various parts of the world had given different names to his ancestors. One name was especially difficult to pronounce and remember: "*Allium Sativum*"! Little Garlic thought, I'll never remember this name. It's just too difficult. I like "Little Garlic" the best!

Little Garlic was listening with all his head and heart.

He learned many interesting things about himself. He learned that he had something called "power" and that he was actually a bulb made of many cloves, each wrapped in a thin wrapper. His bulb had come from a mother bulb that had grown, regrown, and multiplied from the original bulb for thousands of years. He learned that each garlic has within itself all the memory from ancient times.

He was excited to learn that he had many relatives in different parts of the world, and many of them looked different from each other.

Onion began to think that all this new information

might be too much for his little friend. So, he asked Little Garlic if he wanted to know an ancient tale about how it all started.

Little Garlic was so thrilled to finally hear the real story that he jumped on Onion's lap and put his head right on Onion's chest.

Onion began to share this story.

"It's been said that a Chinese princess who was one of the wives of a Tibetan king had the secret of the elixir of life."

"Onion, what's elixir?"

"Well, elixir means the secret that makes people live forever," Onion explained.

"Okay, I got it."

Onion continued with the story. "One day, a thief stole the elixir and drank it. The king's soldiers went and searched everywhere for him. They finally caught him and brought him to be punished before everyone. It is said that in the spot where the thief was killed, a drop of his blood fell to the ground, and in that spot a garlic grew. That's how people figured out the secret of the elixir of life.

19

"This is how the story is told. No one from Tibet who hears this story really thinks that's how garlic was created, but they understand its real meaning."

Little Garlic, who was listening to every word of the story, asked Onion, "What's the real meaning?"

"You see, little fella, in the old days, people who were wise would tell important things or secrets in stories. Other people who wanted to know the secrets of life and how to have real happiness would think deeply about the meaning of the stories and appreciate their value, while others thought of the stories as just fairytales.

"As we go on our journey, I will share with you other stories like this—how wise people through time have told secrets in stories that seem like fairytales to other people.

"Let me ask you, little fella, do you know what this story really means?"

Little Garlic said, "Let me think. I don't know. Can you tell me?"

"Gladly. It tells us that garlic is an elixir for long life. Humans have discovered that garlic has many,

many benefits for a long life because it has rejuvenating powers."

"What's rejuvenating?"

Onion said, "It has many meanings. Think of it this way—it's like the sun that gives energy and new life every day, allowing every living thing to grow and be strong.

"So, now you know how much your ancestors and relatives have been valued for thousands and thousands of years. Next time someone calls you 'Stinky,' you just remember this story!"

"I will, Onion," promised Little Garlic.

Onion smiled, "I know you will. But it's not enough for other people to know your value. You have to find out for yourself. If you don't, you'll never be confident like your ancestors.

"So, are you ready for the journey?"

"Yes, Onion, I'm one hundred percent ready. This is so exciting!"

"As you go on the journey, little by little you will meet your relatives and discover the places where your ancestors have lived. You will also find friends along the way and hear from them little secrets about their journey."

Onion noticed that the sun was setting, and it would be best to wait until morning to share the story of Magic Wind with Little Garlic.

"There's a secret I would like to share with you, but it's getting dark now and we can both use a good night's rest so we can get ready for the morning. What do you think, little fella?"

Little Garlic nodded sleepily. "You've shared so much with me today, and it's a good idea to rest. Maybe I'll dream of my ancestors tonight."

"Okay, little fella. Now, close your eyes and feel how special you are and let this wonderful feeling spread through you and let it settle in your heart and eyes."

Smiling, Little Garlic closed his eyes and said, "Thank you for all the stories, and thank you for being my friend, Onion. I can't wait for tomorrow. Good night."

"Good night little fella. Sweet dreams."

Magic Wind

"GOOD MORNING, little fella! I hope you had good dreams last night."

"Good morning, Onion! I had wonderful dreams, all about my ancestors. They were all so kind to me. I have so much energy today. I'm ready to go on the journey!"

"Now that you're ready, I'll share this important secret with you, but you must promise not to tell anyone about it until it's time," Onion said.

"I don't know anyone, Onion, so how can I tell anyone anything?"

Onion said, "You will meet many, many friends along the way, but you must keep this secret until you're one hundred percent sure they're ready to hear it. It's important to keep secrets safe."

"Okay Onion, I promise."

"Here's the deal," Onion said. "Anyone who wants to go on this journey must get to know Magic Wind and discover Secret Star."

"Oh no, Onion! I was so ready to go on this journey, but now you're telling me that I have to do something so difficult!"

"It's not difficult at all. If you really want to go on your journey, you'll get to know Magic Wind, and with the help of Magic Wind, you'll discover your Secret Star."

"This is so exciting! I really, really want to go on this journey. What do I have to do?"

"Listen carefully," Onion said. "Do you remember the little boy who took me to his house when I was all by myself?"

Little Garlic replied, "Yes, I remember. You became good buddies."

"That's right! My friend took me outside in the back yard every morning before he left for school so I wouldn't be all by myself in the house. I sat outside under the sun and listened to the birds, watched the squirrels chase after each other, felt the gentleness of the breeze, and smelled the fragrance of the flowers. It was so nice to be outside while I waited for my friend to come home from school.

"One day when I was outside, a pumpkin rolled around and stopped right in front of me. He asked who I was and why I was all alone.

"I told him that I wasn't really alone and that I had a best friend. I told him that my friend went to school in the morning and came home after school. Then we spent the rest of the day together.

"Pumpkin said, 'I see, you have a very good buddy indeed!'

"I said, 'Yes, we're best friends!' Then I told him about my friendship with the little boy.

"I told him that the boy had brought home many books from the library, with stories about my origins, ancestors, and relatives—similar to the stories I've told you about your origins, ancestors, and relatives.

"After listening very carefully to my story, Pumpkin said, 'That's all fine and dandy, but you just can't sit around day after day without finding out who you really are and where you came from. Books are a good way to learn, but you need more than books to discover how unique you really are.'

"'Well,' I thought to myself, 'who does he think he is, telling me that I don't know who I am? What does he know about me anyway?' It just sounded strange to me. Then I thought, 'But what if he knows something I don't know!'

"So I asked him to explain what he was talking about. Pumpkin started to tell me his own story, and it began much the same way as ours do.

"It was Pumpkin who told me about Magic Wind and Secret Star. It all sounded weird at the beginning, but as I went on my journey, I found out how important they really are.

"Do you remember how the wind came and brought you here where you were left all by yourself and you didn't know anyone? It was Magic Wind! And do you remember how scared and lonely you were? That same Magic Wind that brought you here also brought me here right next to you!

"It was no accident that Magic Wind brought me

here. No sir! Your Secret Star knew how lonely and unhappy you were. When you had reached the end of your rope and you cried out for help, your Secret Star whispered to Magic Wind to bring me to you.

"At the beginning of our journey, we don't know too much about Magic Wind. Sometimes we blame it for taking us to places we don't like, or to places where we don't have fun. Or, maybe we're just scared because we don't know where it's going to take us.

"But there are also times we enjoy the places Magic Wind takes us because we have fun and become happy."

"Onion, I'll go anywhere as long as you're with me."

Onion paused a little and said, "No matter how happy or unhappy it makes us, we have to go on with our journey to find real happiness. Do you know why?"

Little Garlic said, "I don't know, but I really want to know! Please tell me."

"We must continue with our journey," answered Onion, "because everyone's story is unique, and every-one has a special gift—a hidden treasure. When we discover this gift, we feel whole and complete. And we don't feel lonely, sad, or insecure anymore."

"What does 'insecure' mean, Onion?"

"It means that we don't feel safe inside ourselves. We don't feel sure of who we are and what we say and do."

"Onion, it must be wonderful not to feel insecure!"

"That's true! But most of us, if not all of us, feel insecure at one time or another. It's important not to feel discouraged if we feel we're not making progress. Each step we take along the journey gives us more strength. As awful as we may feel some days, we have to have hope that we will feel better, and we will discover our special gift. Remember, never, ever give up hope!"

"Thank you, Onion. I'm beginning to understand. I'll try very hard to remember this important lesson."

"Yes, it is an important lesson," Onion said in a tender voice and continued, "and I'm glad you're paying close attention to what I'm saying. The journey teaches us many, many things about ourselves and many things about everything that we come across.

"Magic Wind knows where to take us, but we have to really want to go on the journey and have a little trust in Magic Wind. Those who don't want to discover their special gift won't become friends with Magic Wind and won't get to know their Secret Star.

"You see, little fella, Magic Wind and Secret Star are connected! You'll understand this as we go along the journey. Whatever I say about Magic Wind and Secret Star won't make much sense to you now.

"I had to go on this journey to find out for myself. Along the way, I met many wonderful friends. I also met a few who were not so nice. But I learned a lesson from each one of them. That's how I got to understand many things about myself and about others."

"Onion, I really want to become friends with Magic Wind and discover my Secret Star."

Onion, in a reassuring voice said, "Now that you really want to know Magic Wind and discover your Secret Star, it will all work out. I'm pretty sure Secret Star knows what's in your heart.

"This is a new day, and I can feel Magic Wind coming our way. Before Magic Wind gets here, you need to learn how to open your seven wings and ride along with it.

"Just watch how I open my wings. This is how it works. Focus in your heart, take a deep breath, push the air out and feel it move through your seven cloves, and you will feel the translucent wings that cover your cloves open up. These are your wings. When Magic Wind comes, you'll be able to fly smoothly along with it."

"Are you ready?" Onion asked.

"My wings are open, Onion. This is magic!"

"Here we go! Let's see where Magic Wind is going to take us and what we're going to learn today."

The Story of Lotus Blossom

ONE MORNING when Little Garlic and Onion were hanging out and enjoying the vast variety of flowers that surrounded them, Magic Wind came along and swiftly took them far away close to a swamp.

Little Garlic noticed something he had never seen before.

"Onion, who is this beauty with so many wings— such colors, such loveliness, such gracefulness!"

Onion, who had traveled far and wide and knew just about everything, said, "Why don't we go and ask her?"

"I'm too shy; I'm scared to ask; she's so awesome. Can you please ask her?"

"All right," Onion said.

"I beg your pardon, would you mind telling my friend here your name?" For a moment, nothing stirred; nothing was heard. There was total silence and stillness.

Then a gentle voice sweetly said, "They call me Lotus Blossom." Little Garlic, who was trying very hard to overcome his shyness, suddenly blurted out, "How did you become so beautiful?"

Lotus Blossom sighed and in a tender voice replied, "The swamp made me beautiful!"

Little Garlic, who didn't want to seem rude or offend Lotus Blossom, whispered to Onion, "How can such a dirty, stinky swamp create such beauty?"

Lotus Blossom, who heard Little Garlic's whisper, said, "Come here closer to me and I'll tell you my story."

Little Garlic hesitated to go closer, afraid that Lotus Blossom would think he was stinky and wouldn't like him. But he thought that if he didn't muster up enough courage now, he might not have another chance. Besides, he had to find out if Lotus Blossom was like so many others he had met. Then he thought,

'So what if she thinks I'm stinky. It only means she doesn't know me.' So, he finally got up enough courage, opened his seven wings, closed his eyes, and spun around until he was at the edge of the swamp right next to Lotus Blossom.

As he opened his eyes, he saw Lotus Blossom looking at him in amazement. She said, "How did you do that? That looks so cool. Is it magic?"

Little Garlic said, "Onion has taught me how to do this. He has taught me everything I know. Before I met Onion, I was stuck in one place and had no friends. But Onion taught me about my wings, how to use them, and how to fly along with Magic Wind."

Lotus Blossom was impressed by what she heard. She thought of her own experience with Magic Wind and decided that there must be a reason that Magic Wind had brought this little fella here.

She asked, "What is your name and who is Onion?"

Little Garlic said, "This is my friend, Onion. He calls me 'little fella' and sometimes he calls me Little Garlic. I guess it's because I'm so small."

"I'm pleased to meet you both."

Little Garlic said, "I don't mean to sound ignorant, but I don't understand how a dirty swamp made you so beautiful. Do you think you could explain this to me?"

"Of course! If you like, you can jump onto one of my petals, and we'll go around the swamp and I'll tell you my story. That is, if Onion doesn't mind staying by himself for a while."

Totally excited at this opportunity, Little Garlic said, "Oh, that would be so wonderful, I'm sure Onion won't mind, will you?" Onion smiled and said, "Of course not, little fella. Go and enjoy yourself."

When Lotus Blossom heard this, she said, "Okay, jump onto this petal and I'll ask my sister lotuses to come, wave their petals, and take us around." She gave a signal with her petals and all her sisters came their way, moving their petals to create gentle waves that took Lotus Blossom and Little Garlic around the swamp.

"Okay, now that we're on our way, I'll share a little bit of my story with you. In this ancient land where I was born, I'm considered to be a sacred flower. Actually, in many cultures the lotus is considered a sacred flower."

"What does 'sacred' mean, Lotus Blossom?"

"It's a little difficult to explain, but I'll give it a try. It means that something, or someone, is considered to be very, very special, and deserving of love and respect."

"Thank you, Lotus Blossom."

"You're very welcome!"

Lotus Blossom continued with her story, "Teachers bring their students here to tell them about me so they can better understand their own spiritual journey. Sometimes, I'm compared to the sun because at nightfall I close my petals and go under the water, and at dawn I come up above the water and open my petals again—like sunrise and sunset, a new life every day!

"Some say the lotus represents purity of heart—a message that wise people like to teach their students so they can learn about the goodness of their own heart."

Lotus Blossom noticed that Little Garlic looked a little puzzled and confused. "Don't worry that you don't understand all that I'm saying. Just listen for now and I'm sure as you go along your own journey, you'll understand what I'm sharing."

Little Garlic was relieved to hear that he didn't have to understand everything that Lotus Blossom was saying, but he paid extra attention to make sure he heard everything.

"As I was saying, teachers use my story as a way to teach their students the importance of keeping a loving and kind heart. They teach them how it's possible to live a life of goodness under very difficult conditions. They say that you can change all the bad things—just like the filth in the swamp—and become loving and beautiful."

"This is very interesting, Lotus Blossom, but it's a lot to understand."

"Yes, it is," she said in a kind and gentle voice. "Don't worry. It will all come together for you as time goes on."

"I hope so. Will you tell me more?"

Lotus Blossom continued, "I hear a lot about how tough it is for humans to become loving and good.

44

They say they have to work at it every day. But I wonder how many of them would be willing to stay even for a day in this swamp that's filled with waste from the surrounding villages that attracts all kinds of bugs and flies!"

Little Garlic became sad at what Lotus Blossom was sharing and said, "I'm so sorry to hear about your hardships day after day!"

Lotus Blossom looked tenderly at Little Garlic and said, "What keeps me going is my love for the sun. Every morning I come up from under the water in the hope of seeing the sun. I focus all my attention on the sun so that my petals and leaves absorb the loving rays of the sun. This makes me feel all the goodness of life. When the sun sets, I go under the water until sunrise, and then I come up again. Looking forward to seeing the sun keeps me going."

Lotus Blossom paused for a minute then continued sharing her story, "Not all lotuses live in swamps. Some are grown in ponds by humans for their health benefits such as rejuvenation and mental clarity."

Little Garlic said, "Onion told me about rejuvenation when he was telling me about my ancestors. You have this power, too!"

Lotus Blossom said, "I'm glad Onion shared this with you so you can appreciate the gift that you've been given.

"I have to say, those lotuses that live in ponds don't have to endure these tough conditions like we do. But I'm not sure if they're better off than we are. We nurture love and hope in our heart every day to endure life in the swamp. Otherwise, we wouldn't have the strength to overcome the difficulties."

"This is so interesting, Lotus Blossom. Now, I understand much better what Onion has told me about hope. He said, never ever stop having hope!"

In a reassuring voice, Lotus Blossom said, "Yes, hope is indeed very important in life."

Lotus Blossom continued with her story and said, "People say that lotus calms the heart and makes the mind strong. Both are important ingredients for the spiritual journey. There are many stories about the benefits of the lotus."

Little Garlic tried very hard to understand what

Lotus Blossom was saying, but he didn't know anything about "purity of heart," "mental clarity," and "spiritual journey." This was a whole new vocabulary for him and a whole new world!

"What is a spiritual journey, Lotus Blossom? Onion and I are on a journey."

"There are different types of journeys. A spiritual journey is about trying to learn about yourself, and to be good and kind and true. You can do this in different ways, even while going from place to place and learning to see the goodness and beauty in all things."

Lotus Blossom paused for a moment, then said, "Let me ask you a question, do you know what you look like?"

"No, I don't!" said Little Garlic.

"Would you like to get a glimpse of yourself?"

"I really, really would!"

"Okay, slide onto this other petal very carefully, gently bend forward, and take a look."

Little Garlic did exactly what Lotus Blossom said and looked down, but he couldn't see very clearly what he looked like. He only saw a blurry image.

Nonetheless, it was a very exciting moment for him; it was the first time he had gotten any idea of what he looked like.

Lotus Blossom said, "You know, this isn't what you really look like."

"It isn't?" exclaimed Little Garlic.

"No, you look very different. We can't rely on murky water to see what we really look like. I don't depend on this murky water to see myself."

"Lotus Blossom, you don't look anything like what this water shows. That's not how I see you. You are so beautiful!"

Looking at Little Garlic in the sweetest way possible, Lotus Blossom said, "You've said something very important. I see my beauty in the eyes of those who look at me lovingly, just as you have today. It's the love in my heart that those who look at me lovingly see!"

Little Garlic was happy that Lotus Blossom understood how he saw her.

"I've shared a lot with you today and I can tell that you have many questions. I'm sure that as you go on your travels and learn more about yourself, you'll come to understand things more clearly."

Lotus Blossom noticed that the sun was setting and gently said, "It's getting late, let's get back and not keep Onion waiting."

She signaled her sister lotuses to wave their petals and guide them back to land, where Onion was patiently waiting for their return.

"Before we say goodbye," Lotus Blossom said in a reassuring voice, "I want you to know that you are very special. Never let anyone tell you that you're not. Just like me, you have an important message to share with others."

As they arrived where Onion was waiting for them, Lotus Blossom said, "It's been wonderful to get to know you. I know we will both remember this day and remain friends forever, even if we don't see each other again. Remember, real friendships never end.

"The sun is about to set, and it's time for me to join my sister lotuses and go to our special place under the water. Take good care of yourself. So long, Little Garlic!"

"I will always remember you, Lotus Blossom. You have taught me so much. You have so much wisdom and you are a really good friend. I hope one day I will also have a special story to share with someone who really needs it. So long, Lotus Blossom!"

Little Garlic opened his seven wings, whirled around, and joined Onion on land. He watched Lotus Blossom join her sister lotuses as they all disappeared under the water.

"Did you have a good time, little fella?"

"It was so wonderful! I don't even know how to explain it. Lotus Blossom has a lot of wisdom, but I'm not sure I can explain it. I just know I felt it. She said it will all become clear as I continue on my journey."

"That's right, it will all become clear. It's getting dark, what do you think if we get a good night's rest after such an exciting and important day? Who knows where Magic Wind will take us tomorrow!"

In an excited voice Little Garlic said, "Onion, I got a glimpse of what I look like, but it wasn't clear at all!"

Onion smiled and asked, "How did it feel?"

"It was pretty amazing! Lotus Blossom said that as I continue on my journey, I'll be able to see myself much better."

Onion said, "Lotus Blossom is indeed very wise."

"Okay, Onion. I'm ready to get a good night's rest."

"Good! Make yourself comfortable, close your eyes and feel all the beauty and goodness you experienced today. Feel it in your heart and in your wings. Rest deeply and sweet dreams, little fella."

"Good night, Onion. I'm filled with so much goodness, hope, and love. Thank you for being my friend."

The Story of Rambutan

I T WAS NO ACCIDENT that after Little Garlic met Lotus Blossom and was stunned by her beauty, that one day, Magic Wind took him and Onion to a very different place. It was a long journey; they passed over mountains, rivers, oceans, and landed somewhere that seemed quite strange to Little Garlic.

He looked around him and became scared. "Onion, Onion, what are these creatures around me? I'm scared. They're so ugly. Are they going to hurt us? There are so many of them!" Little Garlic exclaimed.

Onion knew why Magic Wind had brought them there. He knew that his little friend still had to learn many important lessons that would be useful if he wanted to discover his own special treasure; and this was to be a very important lesson.

"Do not fear!" Onion said. "Do you remember when we first met, I said that everything, and I mean absolutely everything, has a special gift—a special reason for being, and that they have a special secret that can guide us to discover our own secret?"

"Yes, Onion, I remember," Little Garlic answered.

"Good! So, if we really want to discover this, it's important that we pay attention to everything that's around us. We need to really look at them and see who they really are. Each creature has a special gift, a special message for us, but we must look at them in a special way."

"What's this special way?" Little Garlic asked.

Onion said, "I'm pretty sure Magic Wind brought us here for a reason, perhaps to experience this special way of seeing."

Little Garlic said, "Onion, please explain everything slowly. I don't understand what you're telling me. How can these ugly things have a special gift? I don't want to be near them."

Onion understood that this was going to be an important lesson in the growth of his little friend. Just then, they heard a voice say, "Pardon me, may I introduce myself?"

Little Garlic got even more scared and hid behind Onion.

"Don't be frightened little one. I know I may seem ugly, but I have a beautiful and lustrous interior, and my scent is sweet."

Little Garlic wasn't sure what to do, but he decided that since Onion was with him, it was probably safe to come around and hear what this creature had to say.

The creature said, "Thank you for trusting me little one. My name is Rambutan. Do you know what it means?"

Little Garlic politely said, "No, I don't."

"Well, in this part of the world, the word 'rambu' means hair, and as you can see, I have lots of it! We are called by different names in different parts of the world. Here, in this beautiful luscious land we're called Rambutan.

"My ancestors lived far from here. It is said that people from far-away lands brought them here, while others took them to other far-away places. We are all over the world. Now think—if we are so ugly and scary, why would people bother to take us all over the world?"

Little Garlic didn't know what to think nor what to say. He just looked perplexed and uneasy.

Rambutan, seeing Little Garlic's discomfort, said, "You know little one, my friends and I are used to others reacting this way when they see us. When we were little, about your age, it used to bother us, but we slowly learned that it is a gift that we look the way we do. We know that we look ugly and scary at first, but our beauty is inside and has to be discovered. There's a reason that we are the way we are. Maybe if I showed you, you would be able to figure it out."

Bravely Little Garlic said, "I'm so sorry for the way I reacted. I'd be grateful if you would show me, so I can learn."

"Very well then, I'm happy to show you," answered Rambutan. By now, all the rambutans had gathered around and were watching attentively to what was about to happen. Little Garlic tried not to display any fear at the sight of so many rambutans so close by.

Rambutan stepped forward and in one swoop opened his hairy cover and displayed his beautiful translucent interior.

Little Garlic looked amazed and stunned at what he saw. He was in awe. He hadn't seen anything like it before. It was like a shimmering window through which you could see pure light. It was amazing! It was wonderful!

"So, what do you think, little one?" Rambutan asked.

Little Garlic was quiet. He was dazed. He needed time to figure out what was going on inside himself. Tears began to swell up in his eyes. He couldn't figure out why he was so overwhelmed with emotion.

Onion knew what was going in his little friend. Rambutan could also tell the upheaval that was going on in Little Garlic.

To give Little Garlic time to collect himself, Rambutan went on, "When we were very young like you, and were still attached to our mother tree, one day a couple of strangers came close to us. They kept looking up at where we were, all hanging from different branches. One of them said, 'Look what we've found! There are so many of them, I bet if we wait long enough, they'll all become ripe, and we can take them to the market and sell them for a good price.' The other one agreed, 'Let's just hang around here until it's time to pick them.'

"We didn't exactly know what they were saying, but we all understood that they were going to take us away from our mother tree. We were scared and didn't know what to do. We felt our mother tree's sadness and we too became very sad. It felt like our happy family was going to be split up, and our carefree days were going to end.

"Many days passed, and the two strangers stayed close by. They inspected us every day to see if we were ready to be picked. Then, one day, one of them said, 'I think today is the day. If we wait longer, they'll become too ripe and we won't be able to sell them for a good price. Let's start picking them.' The other one said, 'I don't think they're quite ready, but I guess you know better.'

"Our hearts sank; we closed our eyes and held tight

to our mother tree, fearing what was about to happen. But all of a sudden, to our amazement, a strong wind blew our way. It was so strong that it lifted the two strangers off their feet and threw them far away from us. They got so frightened that they ran off and never came back. As soon as the strangers fled, the wind stopped. We were so thankful and overjoyed that we were safe, that we all started crying together."

Little Garlic innocently asked, "Was it Magic Wind that came and saved you?"

Onion was proud of Little Garlic's question. Rambutan answered, "Yes, it was, but we didn't know anything about Magic Wind then. We heard about Magic Wind later."

Little Garlic said, "How did you hear about Magic Wind? Did you hear it from my friend, Onion? Onion told me about Magic Wind when we first met."

Rambutan smiled and said, "Well, everybody gets to know about Magic Wind in a special way. After the strangers ran away, our mother tree told us about Magic Wind and how it had come along to save us. She also said that when we are ready to live our own lives and be separated from her, Magic Wind will come along and help us again. We didn't really understand what mother tree was saying at the time, but we listened very carefully.

"And so, one day, when we were still on the branches of our mother tree, we felt a wind come our way and shake the branches. We all fell to the ground and didn't know what to do. One of my siblings said, 'Do you remember that our mother tree told us that when we are ready to be on our own, Magic Wind will come along and help us?'

"Well, we understood that we were to be on our own, but we didn't know what we were supposed to do now that we were separated from our mother tree. So, we stayed by ourselves on the ground close to our mother tree day after day until one day, a group of people came along and sat nearby.

"One of them, who looked much older than the others, said, 'We have arrived at an important place on our journey. Do any of you know why this is important? Each of the younger ones said something. They all tried to be clever. The older one, who we found out was their teacher, pointing at us asked, 'Would any of you like to look like any of them?' They all said that we looked ugly and they never wanted to look like us.

"The teacher asked, 'Do you remember when you all ganged up and made fun of the kid in your class whom you said was ugly? This is the reason we're here today. I'm going to ask one of these little fellows to step forward so I can show you how special everything and everyone is.'

Rambutan said, "I was curious to find out, so I stepped forward and volunteered. The teacher pointed at me and said that I had a treasure hidden inside of me. She came closer and closer until she was right in front of me, then asked if I had ever seen what's inside of me. I had no idea what she was talking about. I said, "No, I haven't."

"'Then may I show you?' asked the teacher.

"'Yes,' I eagerly agreed.

"With a quick movement of her hand, as if a wind was turning me about, my chest opened and split in two and there it was: a beautiful translucent heart with light shining through it! The kids' eyes were glued on me and they didn't say a word.

"A few moments passed, then the teacher asked them if they now understood the reason they were there. The kids looked at each other, then one of them said that he was ashamed for having been so nasty to that kid in their class, the one they called 'ugly.' The other kids agreed and said that this was a very important lesson for them.

"The teacher then asked, 'Which one of you can say for sure, that you have such a beautiful and translucent interior?' The kids all lowered their heads and didn't say a word. The teacher said, 'Very well, now that you have learned this important lesson, you must pay attention, and treat all things and everyone with respect from now on. The way to know if you're on the right track, is to ask yourself, how do I want to be treated?' When you treat all things with respect, you grow the seed of goodness in yourself. Then, your heart will be as translucent and beautiful as Rambutan's.'"

Rambutan looked at Little Garlic with a smile and said, "If it hadn't been for that teacher, we wouldn't have discovered our own treasure. That teacher showed us how to see and value ourselves. Who knows, if she hadn't opened up my chest, whenever anyone told us we were ugly, we would have believed them. What the teacher taught her students made us understand that we had a special purpose in life. Since then, many teachers have brought their students here to teach them this lesson."

Little Garlic was paying close attention to Rambutan's story. He understood why he had been overwhelmed with so many different emotions. He said, "I really feel ashamed of myself for saying that you were ugly. I should have known better. Before meeting Onion, I thought I didn't matter because everyone called me 'Stinky' and no one wanted to be around me.

"Onion has been teaching me how to look at things so I can see their special gift and purpose. I guess I hadn't learned this lesson yet. I'm so sorry for having been so rude, and insensitive."

"Don't worry about it." Rambutan answered kindly. "This was an important reminder; besides, it takes time to learn these things. Important lessons sometimes come through painful experiences. You're still very young, but I see that you have a tender heart and want to learn."

Little Garlic said, "Thank you Rambutan for being so kind and for sharing your story. It really helped me remember how I felt before meeting Onion."

"You're most welcome, little one. I know you will learn a great deal as you continue on your journey."

Rambutan looked up at the sky, then back at Little Garlic and Onion and said, "It's getting dark, would you like to rest here for the night?"

Gratefully, Onion and Little Garlic accepted the invitation and thanked Rambutan and his siblings for their kind hospitality and wished them a good night.

When they were alone, Onion asked Little Garlic how he was feeling.

Little Garlic said, "I feel better now, but I felt awful at one point. I was really embarrassed and ashamed of how I behaved. This was a day that I think I will always remember. You were right, Magic Wind had a big lesson in mind for me to learn!"

"Yes, I believe so," agreed Onion. "The important thing is that you've learned something that will be with you wherever you go and whatever you see. As Rambutan said, sometimes important lessons are learned through painful experiences. And, sometimes through nice ones, too, like when you saw Rambutan's beautiful translucent heart!"

"Yes, that was awesome—what a magical experience!" exclaimed Little Garlic.

"It's getting late now, what do you think if we got a good night's rest?"

Little Garlic said, "I would like that, but may I first ask you a question?"

"Of course, it's okay," Onion said.

"You know Onion, when Rambutan opened his chest, it was so beautiful, and just as he promised, a sweet scent came out of his heart. That was really special. Is the rough ugly coat of Rambutan to protect his interior from harm?"

"Yes, little fella, it's to protect it from harm. That translucent heart is so fragile that if it were exposed for long, it wouldn't even last for a day. I'm so proud of you for thinking deeply about this."

"Thank you, Onion. I hope I didn't embarrass you today."

"Of course not. I know what's in your heart. These are all learning experiences."

"Thank you, Onion."

"Good night, little fella. Sweet dreams."

"Good night, Onion. Thank you for being my friend."

The Story of Caterpillar

ONE DAY, when Little Garlic and Onion were leisurely spending the day near a stream where wildflowers grew, Little Garlic noticed something really beautiful flying around, going from one flower to another and circling back around them. He couldn't figure out what it was. He said, "Onion, look, look, what's that flying around?"

Onion smiled and said, "It's a butterfly!"

Little Garlic looked puzzled. He couldn't figure out how this thing was able to fly around whenever and wherever it wanted when they had to wait for Magic Wind to take them from place to place.

Onion realized that Little Garlic had no way of knowing how a butterfly becomes a butterfly! He thought this would be a good time to share with him the story of the caterpillar. "Well little fella, while we're waiting for Magic Wind to take us to our next destination, let me share a story that I think you'll find interesting.

"One day, when I was waiting for Magic Wind, I noticed something small, skinny, and long crawling on the rough ground, looking as if it was having a hard time. I was worried about it, and I asked if it needed help. I explained that it could climb up on one of my Onion wings and go with me wherever Magic Wind would take us, and it wouldn't have to crawl on the ground."

"The crawling creature looked up at me, quite surprised, and said, 'That would be so wonderful. I just need to get somewhere where I can eat leaves or other things so I can fly.' I became puzzled. I thought to myself, 'What kind of a story is this? How can anyone fly just by eating leaves or other things?' It didn't make any sense to me. But because I didn't want to seem rude, I just listened until it finished its story.

"Little fella, this is a very long and unusual story.

Do you really want to hear it"?

Little Garlic eagerly said, "I really do. I want to know how to fly!"

"Okay, little fella. I'll gladly share it with you."

"Thanks, Onion. I can't wait!"

"Here's how the little creature began its story: 'Before I became the way you see me today, I was a tiny little egg. I'm told that my mom was a butterfly and, to keep us safe, she put all her eggs on a big leaf on a big tree with lots of branches and leaves where she knew we would be safe and would be able to eat and eat and grow up to be just like her. Well, there we were, a bunch of tiny little eggs. Sometime later we hatched and became caterpillars. We ate and ate and slowly grew and grew. We all looked alike!

"'Then, one day, a wild wind shook the branch and leaf where we were all staying together. I couldn't hang onto the leaf, and I fell to the ground. I was all by myself. No matter how hard my siblings tried, they weren't able to help me get back up where they were. I didn't know what to do. I was lonesome, hungry, and full of fear. I became hungrier and hungrier.

75

"'I didn't think anyone would ever notice me or even care what happened to me. So, I began to crawl and crawl. From time to time, I would see a beautiful butterfly fluttering around me, and I wondered if it was my mom giving me a message. Just the thought that this was my mom gave me the hope to continue crawling on the ground day after day.

"'When I had lost all hope, suddenly you showed up! I didn't think anyone would offer to help me. But now I feel so lucky! You're going to help me. I don't feel scared and alone anymore. You're so kind and caring. Can we be friends forever?'

"'Yes, of course!' I answered.

"So, just as that creature crawled up on my Onion wing, Magic Wind came along and took us to a beautiful field where the little creature landed on a big bush with huge leaves where it could eat and eat to its heart's content.

"After several days, it slid down the bush and crawled over to me, then whispered in my ear that it was going to share a secret. It said, 'I'm going back up to the bush and stay on that huge leaf for some time.

I'm going to weave a chrysalis—a covering that will go all around me—and I'll stay there until I'm ready for what comes next.' Then it asked me for a special favor."

"What was the special favor?" Little Garlic asked.

"The tiny creature asked me to be patient and wait until it returned. Then added, 'You won't recognize me when I return, but don't forget our promise to be friends forever!' I didn't understand what it all meant, but I promised.

"Many days and nights went by and I stayed awake to keep watch over the tiny creature and the chrysalis that it was weaving. But, one day I fell asleep and when I woke up, I didn't see the chrysalis and became scared, thinking that something bad had happened to my tiny friend. I started blaming myself, feeling guilty that I hadn't been a good friend and I had let it down. All of a sudden, I saw this beautiful butterfly with colorful wings dance around me. As I was looking at its beauty and at how gracefully it moved around me, I heard a sweet little voice whisper, 'It's me, your tiny friend that you helped, the one that used to crawl.'

"I just couldn't believe my eyes. In amazement, I said, 'My tiny friend that used to crawl? Is it really you?'

"'Yes,' came the answer, 'that's how I used to be—crawling and unable to see much of anything except what was right in front of me. Look at me now: I'm free. This is how I was meant to be. I have wings and I can fly in the skies and see so many things. All the hardships I endured were worth the freedom I have now. But if one day I have to tend to some other things, I don't want you to forget that we promised to be friends forever. Wherever you are, know that I'll be with you.'

"You see, little fella, that butterfly that you asked about is that same creature that used to crawl. Wherever I go, she will come along, until the time comes for her to start her own family. I have a sneaky feeling that this is her farewell dance. She wanted you to know her story. She wanted you to know that all her struggles paid off because she never lost hope. She really wanted you to know that."

"I'm glad she wanted me to know her story." Little

Garlic said, deeply moved. "It's such a beautiful story. I'll always remember her."

"I'm sure you will," Onion replied. "And her story is a reminder that whatever we see has a special message for us."

Little Garlic said, "I have a lot of questions."

"Of course, you do. There's a lot of mystery in the story of the caterpillar, and I'm sure you'll discover the mystery on your own journey.

"We've had a wonderful day, but it's getting dark, and it doesn't look like Magic Wind will be coming along, so let's get a good night's rest and be ready for what tomorrow will bring. Close your eyes and let the hopeful story of the beautiful butterfly fill your heart. Tomorrow you can ask me all the questions you have. Sweet dreams, little fella."

"Good night, Onion. Thank you for sharing this beautiful story of hope and thank you for being my friend."

The Story of Morning Glory

I T WAS EARLY MORNING, and Onion had been up for some time waiting for Little Garlic to wake up. He had been thinking of sharing a story from his travels with Pumpkin.

Little Garlic opened his eyes and saw Onion was wide awake. "Good morning, Onion."

"Good morning, little fella. How did you sleep last night?"

"I really slept well. I think I had a lot of dreams."

"Do you remember any of your dreams?"

"I know they were about secrets, but I can't remember them."

Onion wondered if Secret Star had somehow come to Little Garlic's dreams. He decided that maybe if he shared the story of Morning Glory with Little Garlic, the little fella might remember his dream.

"You know, little fella, there's a secret that very few humans have discovered. Most humans just don't even think that it applies to them."

"What is this secret, Onion?"

"The story that I'm about to share with you is very special. Would you like to hear it?"

"Yes, Onion. I really would."

"Why don't we sit here in this beautiful field of flowers and look at their beauty and see how the rays of the sun are gently caressing them, preparing them for the day.

"During my travels with Pumpkin, Magic Wind took us to a village where all the villagers had gathered in front of a flower. They all looked very sad.

"As we were watching, a little boy stopped by and asked why they were so sad.

"One of the villagers told him that they were sad because their beloved flower hadn't opened its petals for days, and they were worried that it was sick, or even worse, that it had died.

"'I'm best friends with the flower,' said the little boy, 'and we're always talking together and sharing secrets. Please let me through, so that I can go and speak with her and see what's going on.'

"Hearing the words of the boy, the crowd moved aside to let him go up and stand close to the flower.

"To the little boy's dismay, he saw that his friend looked very ill. He had never seen her this way before. He couldn't believe his eyes. He stepped closer and closer and put his ear right next to his friend. Seeing how sad she looked, he started crying and whispering to his friend, 'Morning Glory, Morning Glory, what's going on, what's happened to you? Please wake up, please wake up. It's me, your friend.'

"Not a word was heard. Not even a whisper.

"The little boy wouldn't stop crying. No one could calm him. No one could comfort him.

"Now it had become dark, and the villagers had gone home. The boy didn't budge and continued to stand close to Morning Glory, tears rolling down his face, whispering words of endearment to his friend.

"Above, the sky was filled with stars. The little

boy was so very sad, wishing there was more he could do to comfort his friend. As he looked up at Venus shining bright in the sky, he began to pray very hard for his friend. He prayed all night.

"Then, at last, dawn came. The first rays of the sun were beginning to glow across the horizon.

"To the little boy's surprise, Morning Glory began to gently stir. The little boy watched his friend slowly come back to life. He couldn't contain his joy. He placed his head next to Morning Glory and told her that he had never prayed so hard in his life—not even for himself! He told her that he was so happy that his prayers were answered, and this was the best gift he had ever received.

"Morning Glory began to whisper in the little boy's ear about what had happened and how she had become well again. He listened very carefully. The sun was getting brighter and Morning Glory continued to slowly awaken. All her petals were now open. A new day had begun, and all the sadness was washed away.

"After Morning Glory had finished whispering her story, the little boy said to her, 'I'm so sorry that I wasn't here for you when you were so sad. I was sick and had to stay in bed. As soon as I was well again, I came looking for you.'

"Morning Glory, in the sweetest and most tender voice, told her friend, 'I understand. What's important is that you came, and you didn't forget me. If it hadn't been for your love and your prayers, who knows what would have happened to me? I know there's a big lesson in what happened.'

"By now, the villagers had gathered to see how their beloved flower was doing. To their amazement, they saw that Morning Glory was as beautiful and as radiant as ever. To the little boy, who was still standing next to Morning Glory, they said, 'What happened here? This is a miracle!'

"The little boy who had stood watch and had prayed all night began to share what Morning Glory had whispered in his ear.

"He said, 'You see, Morning Glory lives for the sun. Every morning she awakens by the gentle rays of the rising sun and opens her petals to embrace the sun's rays. All day long, she feels embraced by the sun.

When the sun sets, she closes her petals and waits in the hope that the first rays of the sun will embrace her petals again.

"'But day after day when the sun didn't shine, Morning Glory became more and more sad and her petals didn't open to embrace the sun. No one knew about the Morning Glory's sadness, and no one knew that many tears had gathered in her heart because she hadn't been able to open her petals. Her love for the sun was so great that when the sun didn't shine day after day, tears replaced all the hope she had in her heart.'

"Morning Glory had told the little boy that what brought her back to life was the power of his love and prayers for her. She felt the power of the little boy's love so much that the tears that had gathered in her heart began to slowly melt away and she was able to open her petals with the first rays of the sun again."

Little Garlic said, "This sounds like magic!"

"Well, it's something like magic," answered Onion with a smile. "It's because of Strawberry that Pumpkin and I could understand Morning Glory's story."

Little Garlic in a puzzled voice asked, "Who is Strawberry?"

"I'll tell you about her sometime soon. Pumpkin and I learned many nuggets of wisdom from Strawberry. She taught us about true love, and that's how I could understand the friendship between Morning Glory and the little boy."

"I think I understand it, too, Onion," said Little Garlic. "I liked her story a lot."

"I'm glad," Onion replied. "It's an important story about love, friendship, and prayer. Can you see how they're all connected?"

Little Garlic thought hard. Then he said, "Well, Morning Glory loved the sun so much that she couldn't live without the sun. The little boy loved Morning Glory so much that he poured all his love into prayers to bring her back to life. That's how they're all connected, isn't it?"

"That's exactly right!" said Onion. "I'm so proud of you!"

"I have a question, Onion. Did the little boy love Morning Glory because she was so beautiful?"

"This is an excellent question. I don't know what was in the little boy's heart, but it may well be that at first, the beauty of Morning Glory made the little boy notice her, but then they shared a deep friendship that turned into love.

"There are different types of love. As we continue on our journey, you'll discover all this for yourself."

"Thank you, Onion. I'm beginning to understand what you're saying. I guess the little boy was so devoted to Morning Glory that he would do anything to bring her back to life!"

"That's right," Onion said.

Little Garlic said, "How did the little boy know how to pray?"

Onion said, "You're really asking important questions! I'm so proud of you. This question is really difficult to answer, but let me see if I can explain.

"Real prayer comes from our heart. When someone is very important to us and they are in need of help, the power of this is so great that when we pray from deep within our heart for help, we receive an answer.

"This is just one explanation. Prayer is explained

in many different ways by people all over the world.

"Do you have a prayer in your heart, little fella?"

Little Garlic was quiet for a few moments, then said, "I do, Onion, I just remembered my dream! Secret Star told me how to pray from my heart."

"That's wonderful!" exclaimed Onion, glad that sharing Morning Glory's story had helped Little Garlic to remember his dream. "Maybe it's best that you don't tell me what Secret Star told you."

"Okay, Onion. I know you always have a good reason for what you say."

"And now, because it's the end of the day, what would you think if we said a prayer?" Onion asked.

"That's a great way to end the day, Onion. Thank you for suggesting it."

"Why don't we close our eyes and focus deep in our hearts and say a prayer."

Little Garlic said, "Okay, Onion."

After they had silently said their prayers, Little Garlic looked at Onion and said, "That felt wonderful! I prayed exactly the way Secret Star told me, and I felt a tingling in my heart. It felt so good!"

"That's great, little fella," Onion said, pleased. "Now let's get a good night's rest so we can be ready for our next adventure.

"Make yourself comfortable and relax all your wings and open your heart to the light of the stars. Feel the light of the stars gently enfold you and protect you. Feel their love in your eyes and in your heart. Rest lovingly, little fella. Sweet dreams."

"Good night, Onion. Thank you for sharing the story of Morning Glory and the little boy. Thank you for being my friend. I always wake up in the morning hopeful because you are my friend."

The Story of Strawberry

"ONION, where do you think Magic Wind is going to take us today?"

"It's a mystery when Magic Wind will show up, where it's going to take us, and why it's taking us to wherever it's taking us. After all these years, I still don't know. But I do know for sure, there's always a lesson to be learned!

"While we're waiting for Magic Wind, would you like to hear about a story during my travels with Pumpkin? Do you remember Pumpkin?"

Little Garlic said, "You've only told me a little bit about Pumpkin and how you had met him. You told me that he had wanted you to go with him to find out who you were. Can you tell me what happened to Pumpkin and the little boy who was your best friend?"

"I will. That's a long story and I'll share my experiences with Pumpkin as we go along our journey together. Is it okay if I share the story of Strawberry now and save the story of Pumpkin and the little boy for a later time?"

Little Garlic said, "Okay, but please don't forget. I really want to hear about what happened to the little boy who was your friend and your travels with Pumpkin. What's the story of Strawberry?"

Onion began to share with Little Garlic how, during his travels with Pumpkin, Magic Wind had taken them to a strawberry field.

"You know, little fella, during my travels with Pumpkin we went to many countries, saw many amazing things, and saw many different types of people. I could never understand why people hated, hurt, or killed each other. It was so strange to hear about all the fighting that had gone on for such a long time.

"One day, I asked Pumpkin if he knew why people were like that. Pumpkin said that during his own journey, he had discovered the reason, and added, 'Now that you really want to know the reason for all the hate and fighting in the world, Onion, I'll share with you what a very wise man shared with me.'

"The wise man had told Pumpkin that every night before he went to bed, he should focus in his heart and ask Secret Star to guide him. He was to do this every night until he received the answer.

"Pumpkin told me that if I practiced exactly what the wise man had told him, he was pretty sure that I would receive the answer as well. So, I did exactly what Pumpkin told me.

"It was seven days later that Magic Wind came and took us somewhere far away. I could see from above that there were lots of little red dots in a green field. I had never seen anything like that before.

"Then Magic Wind slowed down, and we landed next to what I learned was a strawberry field. It was such a beautiful day. Everything was sparkling with the light of the sun, especially the red strawberries.

"I asked Pumpkin why Magic Wind had brought us here. Before Pumpkin could answer, we heard a sweet little voice say, 'I know the reason. Magic Wind has brought others here as well.'"

Onion smiled and went on, "Well, you can imagine how surprised I was to suddenly hear an angelic voice out of nowhere. I looked around and saw this adorable bright red heart with what looked like green wings on top of its head.

"The voice said, 'My name is Sweetheart and my family name is Strawberry.' I awkwardly said that I was pleased to meet her and then introduced myself.

"She then said, 'Do you know why I'm called Sweetheart?'

"I really loved her name, and I think I fell in love with her as soon as I saw her. I had no clue why she was called Sweetheart. Apologetically, I said that I didn't know, but that I'd really like to know.

"Before she told us her story, she asked a lot of questions. She wanted to know how long I had been traveling with Pumpkin, how long I'd known Magic Wind, and if I had discovered Secret Star.

"I shared my story with her. Then she asked if I had asked Secret Star a question.

"I said that I had. And she said that she knew that Secret Star had guided me to her to find the answer."

Suddenly, in an excited voice, Little Garlic said, "Onion, now I understand what you told me at the beginning of our journey about Magic Wind and Secret Star and how they are connected! Wow, this is so awesome! I'm beginning to understand. I'm so sorry for interrupting you. Please tell me more about Sweetheart."

Onion said, "I'm so glad you're finding the answers for yourself, little fella." He continued, "Listen carefully. This is how Sweetheart told her story. She said that she came from an ancient heritage, and her ancestors were highly regarded and loved by many people in different parts of the world.

"She said that her ancestors were so loved and honored that strawberry designs were carved on top of altars and pillars in churches and cathedrals.

"She added that it's not important to have a place on altars, even on top of the tallest cathedral. What's important, she said, is to find the source of real love in your own heart.

"She went on, 'Those ancient people who knew how to look deeply into things, discovered the reason for the creation of the strawberry. Those wise people knew we were the perfect symbol for love. So we became the symbol for Venus, the Goddess of Love.

"'Those wise people had hoped that by making us the symbol of love, people would look in their own hearts and find the meaning of real love.'

"She explained, 'Strawberry really is the perfect symbol for love. It's shaped like the human heart, it's red on the exterior, and when you open it, it has an interior world hidden from all eyes. Not many people know this, but the human heart holds the biggest secret: the secret to an invisible world.'"

"Invisible world?" Little Garlic asked. "What did Strawberry mean by that?"

Onion said, "I'm not sure if I can explain it, but I'll try. Well, it's a place that can't be seen with these eyes, but through that special place in the heart. It's a place where everything is peaceful, beautiful, and kind. Some call it paradise."

"Wow, that must be such a magical place! I bet no one calls anybody 'Stinky' there!" Little Garlic exclaimed.

"That's right." Onion responded and continued, "Now listen carefully, little fella. Strawberry told us some very important things, but they can be difficult to understand. Are you up for it?"

Little Garlic sat up straight and said, "As long as you're right here with me, Onion, I am."

"This is what she said, 'People continue to this day to hate and fight each other. Not many people search for the real answer to human suffering. The wisest people, who discovered this secret, shared it with others, but not many people have made an effort to understand for themselves.

"'It's not enough to tell people about things. They have to want to find out for themselves. Hearing about something is the beginning of a search. It's like a sign on the road. Many people may see the same sign, but not many want to go to where it points. Hearing about the meaning of things is a sign; it's not the destination. You have to travel to the destination to know what it's all about!'"

Onion paused and looked at Little Garlic. Gently he said, "Do you understand what Strawberry meant by this?"

Little Garlic was thinking hard. At last, he said, "It's just like you've been telling me, Onion! You can tell me things, but the best way to learn is by experiencing them myself."

Onion smiled. "Well done! That's exactly right."

Little Garlic looked very proud of himself. "What else did Strawberry say to you?"

"She told us, 'Unless you experience for yourself real love, and by real love, I mean experiencing the deepest love possible, you won't know what it feels like by simply hearing about it.

"'If you hadn't come here and met me and my sister strawberries, would you have known what I looked like just because you heard about me? Of course not!

"'When people are guided here, it means they are ready to know about the real love that I'm talking about. Discovering this love is the key to end wars, hatreds, and suffering. You are here today because you really want to know about human suffering. This is the first step and as you go on your journey, you will understand what I'm saying.

"'The source of love is in your heart. We can see this love in different ways: like the love of a mother for her child, the love of one person for another, the love between a person and a pet, and so on.

"Strawberry briefly paused and then said, 'Sometimes, we see that this love turns to dislike, hatred, and separation. The source of love in the heart is always there because it's connected to everlasting love. Being aware of this connection and being in touch with it, changes the way we live. When we are mindful of this love, we treat others with kindness, compassion, respect, understanding, and all the goodness that's in our heart.

"'It also helps us not to judge others but see the value in all things.'

"Sweetheart suddenly interrupted her story, looked at me, and asked, 'Now, do you know why you were guided here by Secret Star with the help of Magic Wind?'

"I was totally caught by surprise. I thought maybe she was testing me to see if I was paying attention to what she was saying. I needed time to think.

"I said, yes! I had asked Secret Star to show me why people hated and fought each other. I guess the answer is that we all have to learn how to really love, and be kind and good to each other.

"Sweetheart then asked if I knew why it was so difficult for some people to love.

"I didn't know what to say. In a gentle and kind voice, Sweetheart said, 'That's a long story, but I'm pretty sure you'll discover the answer as you go on your travels. It's getting late and you've traveled a long distance. It's best that you rest here tonight.'

"Pumpkin and I were in awe of Strawberry's wisdom. We thanked her for giving us so much time and for sharing her knowledge with us. Strawberry then looked up at the bejeweled sky and said, 'Look up at the sky and find the brightest star and feel the light of that star in your heart.' She paused for a minute, then said, 'Now, relax and give away all your tiredness and all your thoughts to the gentle breeze of the night.

"'Let the light of the star fill your heart and rest deeply. Tomorrow morning, we will see each other.

"'Good night, friends.'

"Filled with wonder, awe, gratitude, and a feeling of total peace, I said, 'Good night Sweetheart.'

"That was my first day with Sweetheart," Onion said with a smile. "We spent a few more days with her, and each day she taught me many things that I have never forgotten."

Little Garlic said, "Do you think you can teach me what Sweetheart shared with you?"

"Of course, little fella. As we go on our journey, I'll share some of the things I learned from her. I think you'll also learn a lot from her wisdom."

"I hope so. I know I learned so much today! Thank you for telling me about Sweetheart."

"You're very welcome. And you know what? I think the story of Sweetheart was your gift from Secret Star."

"Wow, really? That's amazing!"

Onion looked at Little Garlic and noticing that his young friend looked sleepy, he said, "It's getting late. How about getting a good night's rest?"

Little Garlic welcomed the idea. He was over-whelmed with the story of Sweetheart. He said, "It's a great idea, Onion!"

"Good night little fella. Sweet dreams."

Little Garlic, with a smile on his face, said, "Maybe Sweetheart will come in my dreams tonight. Good night, Onion. Thank you for being my friend."

Little Garlic's Special Dream

L ITTLE GARLIC opened his eyes to the first rays of the sun with a feeling that something special had happened.

Onion had awakened long before Little Garlic. He had been thinking about all that he had learned from Sweetheart and how his life had changed after meeting her.

Little Garlic said, "Onion, are you awake?"

"Good morning, little fella. How did you sleep last night? Did you have any dreams?"

"Onion, I had the most beautiful dream about Sweetheart. Would you like to hear it?"

"Yes, I would. I'd be grateful."

"I was sitting happily in a beautiful field of flowers watching a bumble bee go from one flower to another,

113

when all of a sudden, I heard a sweet voice say, 'Do you want to discover your Secret Star?'

"I looked over and it was Sweetheart! She was exactly as you had described her. She looked at me so lovingly, as if she had always known me.

"It felt like I had known her, too. She said, 'You have tried very hard to find your Secret Star, and you have listened to what Onion has taught you. So, I'm going to show you how to find your Secret Star.'

"'So,' she said, 'look very carefully at what I'm going to show you.' I was scared that I would do something wrong, and she wouldn't tell me about my Secret Star. She saw how worried I'd become, and in the sweetest and most loving voice, said, 'Don't worry, everything will be okay.'

"Then, very slowly, she began to take a deep breath, and, as if a door was opening, she became two halves, and I could see the interior of her heart. It was as if there was another heart inside of her. She pointed to a little dot on top of her heart that looked like the brightest star I'd ever seen. She said, 'You, too, have a luminous point like this in your own heart, and if you focus on it every night before you go to sleep, you will know your Secret Star. Your Secret Star will guide you to your secret treasure.'

"Then she slowly closed the half of her heart that she had opened and became whole again. In a whisper, she said, 'Everyone has this brightest of stars in their own heart, and it's through this star that they can find their own secret treasure and experience true love!'

"As soon as she said this, she disappeared, and I woke up.

"Oh, Onion, I had so many questions to ask her!

"Onion, what do you think about this dream? Do you think it's a true dream?"

In a tender, loving voice, Onion said, "Little fella, you received a very special gift from Sweetheart. She doesn't give away this secret to just anyone. You have to be ready to receive this very important gift.

"You see, Sweetheart can see in everyone's heart and knows the secret in your heart.

"Indeed, you received a very special gift!

"Maybe, one day, Magic Wind will take you to Sweetheart, and you will see her in the magic garden

115

of strawberries. You see, the place where Sweetheart lives is protected from anyone with bad intentions—that is, people who want to do or say bad things. Only those who are good, kind, and sincere, and want to find their own secret treasure are guided to Sweetheart.

"As you know, Sweetheart is the Goddess of Love, and she teaches the sincere ones how to find true love."

"Onion, I'm going to do what Sweetheart showed me in my dream, and maybe Magic Wind will take me to her one day."

"I'm glad you want to do what Sweetheart taught you. I'm sure you'll discover your Secret Star.

"Well! This is a very important message that you received. Would you like to have a quiet day and think about what Sweetheart taught you? How would you feel if we just relaxed and enjoyed this beautiful day?"

Little Garlic, who needed time to absorb what Sweetheart had taught him in his dream, welcomed Onion's suggestion. "This is really a good idea. I'm kind of overwhelmed by my dream, and a quiet day sounds wonderful."

And so Little Garlic and Onion enjoyed their quiet day together. Sometimes they talked, sometimes they were silent.

Little Garlic reflected about his dream, all that he had experienced along the way, and all that he had learned from Onion.

Onion reflected about Little Garlic's dream. He thought that maybe this was Sweetheart's way of letting him know that Little Garlic was coming of age, and that he would soon have to become independent and go on the journey on his own.

Before they knew it, they realized that the day was coming to a close, and the glow of the setting sun was spreading across the horizon. Dusk was setting in.

Onion said, "How was your day?"

"It was an unusual day, but a nice one," replied Little Garlic. "I felt as light as a butterfly. I felt like I could do anything! So much was happening inside of me. I can't explain it. It was good that we had a quiet day and Magic Wind didn't come along to take us anywhere."

"Yes, it was," Onion said with a smile. It really had

been a wonderful day.

Thinking that Little Garlic might be tired, Onion asked, "Are you ready for a good night's rest?"

"Yes, Onion, I am. Thank you for asking."

"Well then, make yourself comfortable and relax. Close your eyes and become aware of your heart. Feel the goodness in your heart and see that bright star that Sweetheart told you is in everyone's heart. Rest in the wondrous feeling of your dream.

"Good night, little fella. Sweet dreams."

"This was such a wonderous day! Good night, Onion. Thank you for being my friend."

The Story of Adam

ONION AND LITTLE GARLIC woke up very early the next morning. They had rested well the night before and were wondering if Magic Wind would come along to take them to a new destination.

Little Garlic eagerly said, "Onion, while we're waiting for Magic Wind, do you think you could share another story that Sweetheart shared with you and Pumpkin?"

"Yes, of course! It's an excellent idea," Onion replied.

"Thank you, Onion."

And then, Onion began to tell a story just as Sweetheart had told it to him.

Sweetheart tells a story

One day, a man who looked like he had made a long journey came along and sat by the garden. He seemed tired and was looking for a resting place for the night.

I went up to the man and asked why he was by himself and why he was so tired. The man said that his story was very long, and it would take many, many days and nights to tell it.

I told him not to worry about how long it takes, that time doesn't mean anything here. I suggested that he first rest for a while, and my sister strawberries would serve him some refreshments. The visitor thanked me for being so understanding. He stretched out his tired legs and made himself comfortable under the shade of the weeping willow tree.

In an instant he fell into a deep sleep, looking peaceful like a little baby. My sister strawberries placed the refreshments within reach of our visitor and went back to the strawberry garden.

I sat nearby waiting for our visitor to wake up. I knew that whoever comes to us is guided by Secret Star for an important purpose. Looking at our visitor, I understood that this was the last part of his long journey.

The sun had set, and the sky was filled with stars when he opened his eyes. He looked around, wondering where he was. Then, noticing that it was already dark, and the stars were out, he sat up and saw me sitting nearby. He started apologizing for having rested for such a long time, but I reassured him again that time doesn't mean anything here.

I offered him the refreshments and he thanked us for our hospitality. He seemed pleased to sip the sweet nectar from the wildflowers and eat the light meal that was prepared for him.

After he had enjoyed the refreshments, he asked if it was a good time to share his story.

I told him yes, we would very much like to hear his story. This is what he said:

Adam starts from the beginning

When I was very young, my entire family and all our neighbors were severely punished by other villagers just because we practiced a different faith. I don't even remember how old I was. All I know is that just before they came to our house, my mom was able to hide me in a corner under a supply area in our barn where our cows were kept. I stayed there for many days and nights, afraid that someone might find me. I didn't know where to go or what to do. The cows became my friends, and each morning before they were let out to the pasture, they shared their milk with me so I wouldn't go hungry. One late afternoon, I heard a few men talking outside the barn. One of them said that he was going to take the cows to the market and sell them in the morning.

I didn't know what would happen to me if they sold the cows. They were my only friends. What was I to do, where was I to go? When it got pitch black that night and I was sure that everyone had gone home, I said goodbye to the cows and thanked them

126

for having been such good friends to me.

Then I started to walk and walk. I had no idea where I was going. I just wanted to get away from these terrible villagers. During the nights I'd walk, and during the days I'd hide under the bushes so no one would see me. Luckily, I made many friends along the way who helped me. The robins offered seeds, the bumble bees offered honey, the squirrels offered acorns, the sparrows offered breadcrumbs, and so on. All these friends and many more gave me hope and kept me from starving.

I don't know how long I traveled. All I know is that when I finally arrived at a safe place, I passed out from exhaustion. This was the first part of my journey!

When I opened my eyes, I saw a beautiful radiant woman with long white hair sitting quietly close by. Noticing that I was awake, she said in the kindest voice, "It looks like you've been traveling for a very long time, my son." As soon as she said this, I began to cry as if a flood of pain was being released from my heart. No matter how hard I tried, I couldn't hold back the tears. She was looking at me as if she had always known me, with the same tenderness that my mom used to look at me. In a comforting voice she said, "You'll be fine, my son. The period of darkness has ended for you. From now on, your journey will be one of light, love, and peace."

Then, she slowly got up, walked over and gently sat down next to me. She looked like an angel in her long white dress and silken white shawl as if she was filled with light; her eyes looked golden. I had never seen anyone like her before. She had the kindest eyes and a most comforting presence.

She said, "After such a long journey, you're probably hungry and thirsty." I said that I was.

She opened a neatly folded embroidered white cloth and offered me bread, fruits, nuts, and sweets, and cool water from an earthen pitcher. She said, "Please enjoy these offerings."

She sat quietly while I ate. After I had finished, I thanked her and told her how much I had enjoyed the meal. I was eager to tell her what had happened to me. As if she could read my mind, she asked me where

I had come from and how long I'd been traveling. I told her everything I could remember. She asked what my parents had called me. I told her I was called Adam.

"Adam," she said, "you are indeed a brave young man! I've been waiting for you. You are a special young man with an important mission! I'm to give you a special gift, one that will give you the secret to peace. After you've had a chance to rest and unwind from your long journey, we'll sit together by the stream and I'll share the gift with you."

Many days passed. Each day, she would bring me a variety of delicious fruits, nuts, bread, and sweets. I had never eaten so well. I spent the days leisurely walking in the fields, exploring the beautiful rolling hills, watching the farmers in the distant fields, or the shepherd with his flock of sheep. When I got tired, I'd sit by the stream to rest. I loved listening to the calming sound of the stream and watching the clear water that gently moved along, giving life to so many flowers and plants. Sometimes, I'd take a nap. The chatter of the birds was comforting. I never felt alone.

In the evenings around sunset, she came around

and asked me about my day and if I needed anything. There was nothing that I needed. She had made sure that I had everything I could possibly need. I didn't have a care in the world. I felt safe and welcomed.

Each night when the stars began to sparkle in the sky, she told me a story about a different star. Night after night, I learned about another star. She told me how people had figured out how to find their way on land and sea by knowing about the stars. It sounded like magic to me, and it was wonderful to fall asleep hearing how special each star was.

One night, when the stars had lit up the sky as if they were big sparkling jewels, she told me about Secret Star. She told me that everything that exists is guided by Secret Star. She said that when I discover my Secret Star, she would tell me about my special gift and the reason I had been guided to her.

Many nights passed. Each night she shared a special story about Secret Star until I'd fall asleep.

Then, one night, I had a dream that I have never forgotten. When I woke up, I knew that I had found my Secret Star, and I knew that this would be my last day with this angelic woman who had looked after me with such tender care for such a long time.

I was totally overwhelmed by my dream. It was so real. I was transported somewhere beyond the stars, beyond everything that I knew. I felt transformed.

Ever since then, each night at dusk and as soon as I see the first stars in the sky, I close my eyes and I see my Secret Star. I'm then transported to that special place in my dream.

Little Garlic and Onion talk about Adam's story

"Adam's story makes me feel so many things," Little Garlic told Onion. "I was scared for him, then sad, then happy when he found his Secret Star. You and Sweetheart were right—it is an important story!"

"I'm glad you think so, little fella."

"So, what happened next? What else did Sweetheart tell you?"

Onion said, "Adam had been talking to Sweetheart for quite a while, and seeing that it was getting dark, Sweetheart suggested that it might be best that Adam gets a good night's rest, and they would continue in the morning."

"Adam told Sweetheart and the sister strawberries how grateful he was for their care and kindness. He wished them all a good night. That's the end of Adam's story for now, I'll share the rest tomorrow."

"Onion, this was a very interesting story, and I'm looking forward to hearing the rest of it. Do you think you could also share stories about Secret Star like the angelic woman had shared with Adam?"

Onion smiled tenderly and lovingly, knowing that his young friend was on his way to discovering something important. He answered, "Of course, I will."

"That's awesome, Onion! Thank you."

"You're welcome, little fella."

Little Garlic was wondering if Adam's dream about Secret Star was like his own, so he asked, "Onion, did Sweetheart tell you about Adam's dream?"

Onion knew that Little Garlic was sincere and wanted to learn as much as he could about Secret Star. He said, "Yes, she shared Adam's dream with us."

Little Garlic asked, "Onion, will you share Adam's dream with me?"

Onion said, "I would be happy to, but at a later time. We've had an interesting and rewarding day. It would be a good idea to get some rest and enjoy the night sky.

"Are you ready for a good night's rest?" Onion asked.

"Yes, Onion, I am. This was another special day!"

"Yes, indeed. Make yourself comfortable and relax. Look up at the sky and see how beautifully the sky is lit up with stars. Find the brightest star and look at it for a few minutes. Now, close your eyes and feel the light of that star in your eyes and in your heart. Feel that light expand and enfold you. Good night, little fella, sweet dreams."

"Thank you for sharing so many important stories with me. Good night, Onion. Thank you for being my friend."

The Flower of Peace

"**G**OOD MORNING, little fella, did you rest well last night?"

"Good morning, Onion. I was a little restless," answered Little Garlic. "It felt like I was half asleep and half awake. The story of Adam kept coming back to me. The way he had lost his family, traveling by himself for such a long time, the friends he had met along the way, and meeting the angelic woman."

Onion thoughtfully said, "Maybe I should have told you the story of the Flower of Peace last night before you rested so you would have gone to sleep with the Flower of Peace in your mind."

"Don't worry about it, Onion. Maybe it was good for me to hear about Adam's hardships to understand a little better about the connection between endurance and peace."

137

Onion was happy to hear that his young friend was beginning to understand life in a deeper way. He said, "That's a wise way to think about things. I'm so proud of you! Would you like to hear about the Flower of Peace now?"

Little Garlic nodded eagerly. "Yes, please, Onion!"

"Good! So, in the morning, Sweetheart and her sister strawberries took some refreshments to Adam. He had been up since sunrise, and he told them that he had never rested so deeply. It felt as if he had come to the end of his long journey.

"Sweetheart had known from the first moment she had met Adam that he had come there because he had fulfilled his mission. She said to Adam perhaps that was true and asked if he would like to share the rest of his story.

"But first, she asked him to please enjoy the refreshments that her sister strawberries had prepared for him.

"Adam expressed his gratitude for the refreshments. While he was eating, Sweetheart told Adam about her own meeting with the angelic woman. Adam was overjoyed to hear the story. Although he had always felt close to the angelic woman and never felt that they had been separated by time and place, he so loved hearing Sweetheart's story. After Sweetheart had finished, she asked Adam if he would like to continue with his story.

"He said yes. This is what Adam said about his last day with the angelic woman."

Adam continues his story

The morning after my dream about Secret Star, the angelic woman came to see me. I knew right away that this was the day that she was going to give me my special gift. We walked slowly together and quietly sat by the stream.

As always, she opened the beautiful clean cloth and offered me an ample breakfast of fruits, nuts, and sweets. She also offered sweet milk from a shiny turquoise jug that she had brought along.

She asked if I remembered the first day we had met and what she had told me. I said that I did. She

139

looked deeply at me and said in a gentle and caring voice that I was now ready to receive the gift and begin the next part of my journey.

Tears swelled up in my eyes; my chest and throat tightened. I wasn't able to say a word. I knew that this was the day of parting. I couldn't bear the thought of separating from her. She had been my family. Was I to leave her? How could I go on without her? How could I be by myself again? The thought of it was more than I could endure.

I could see in her eyes that she felt the pain that I was feeling. She said in a tender, loving voice that I shouldn't worry about this separation and that I would never feel alone again. She said that every separation is difficult at first, but as we go along our journey, we realize that separation is part of growth and completion.

She gave an example that I have never forgotten. She said that if a seed stayed inside the flower or fruit and never separated, it wouldn't have a chance to become a flower or a fruit. She said that all the wisdom and knowledge of the fruit and flower is in the seed. It's important for the seed to experience all the growth cycles for itself to know what it's like to be a flower or a fruit.

She said that this was true for me as well. Unless I went on this journey, I would never discover all that I have inside of me. She said that when the seed is separated, it knows that it has to overcome many obstacles by itself to survive and become a fruit or a flower. At the beginning, the seed depends on the wind or a bird to take it to a fertile place where it can grow. When it's in the darkness under the ground, the seed has hope that one day it will overcome the darkness and be welcomed by the sun's light. It knows that this is the period when it must make every effort to endure the darkness and not to give up. It knows that this is the time to grow roots and become strong, so it can sprout up above the ground and be nurtured by the sun.

Little Garlic makes a connection

Little Garlic, who had been listening very carefully to every word, said, "Onion, I just thought of something! The story of the seed is similar to the story of the caterpillar—how it changed and grew wings so it could fly and be free in the sky! Is that right, Onion?"

Onion smiled. "That's right, little fella. You are learning so well and looking for the deeper meaning of these stories. I'm so proud of you!"

"Thank you, Onion. I'm sorry that I interrupted you. Please continue with the story of Adam."

"Not to worry. I'm glad you're listening and thinking deeply about everything," Onion said, and then went on telling Little Garlic what Sweetheart had told him.

Sweetheart continues Adam's story

Adam understood what the angelic woman was saying and realized that the death of his family and villagers, the hardships that he had endured along the way before meeting her, had been the period of darkness and growth just like the seed's. The time he had spent with her was also similar: she had nurtured him just like the sun does. And so, Adam knew in his heart that he must now continue his journey and fulfill his destiny.

The angelic woman had told Adam that when she was around Adam's age, someone had given her a special gift, and she had been told that one day a young man would come along, and she was to give him this gift. She had told Adam that the message of the Flower of Peace would be Adam's gift to people all around the world. He was to travel from village to village, from city to city, from country to country, and share the message with everyone he met.

I asked Adam if this was the reason he was here. He said that the angelic woman had told him that one day his travels would take him to a secret garden. This was the garden where love is harvested, and when he got there, he should share the story with the Goddess of Love.

This is what I told Adam: "Welcome to the garden of love! You have fulfilled your mission. This is where you will be rewarded for all the work you have done for so many long years. You have spread the message of hope and peace far and wide. This is where you will enter the garden of paradise and be blessed with eternal love."

143

Adam thanked me for the blessing, and I asked him if he wanted to share with all the sister strawberries the special gift that the angelic woman had given him.

Adam told me that he would gladly share the gift. He said that the angelic woman told him that the secret of ending the violence on earth is through the message of the Flower of Peace, and he reached in his pocket and took out a tiny seed. He placed the seed in the palm of his left hand, closed his eyes, took a deep breath from his heart and as he exhaled slowly, he opened his hand, the seed had become pure light. It looked like a heart made of light!

As soon as I saw this, I knew that Adam had been given the great secret to peace on earth. My sister strawberries and I remained quiet until Adam was ready to speak again.

Adam finishes telling his story to Sweetheart

When the angelic woman was about to tell me the story of the Flower of Peace, she opened a tiny blue velvet pouch and took out this same seed and put it in

144

her palm and did exactly what I did just now. I was amazed at what I saw—a seed turned into pure light!

She said, "My story is similar to yours. When I was a child, war broke out in my country and for some reason I got lost and was all alone. I was too young to remember what had happened, but the family who found me in the ruins of our village told me all they knew about my family. The pain of separation from my family never left me, so I decided to start on a journey and find them. I traveled far and wide, but I didn't have many clues to go by—only what I had heard from the family who took me in.

"One day, when I was totally worn out from traveling, I collapsed from exhaustion, thirst, and hunger. A kind old woman found me and cared for me until I was well and strong. For the longest time I had wanted to find out the reason for the violence in the world and to find out why people hated each other. I asked the old woman if she knew. She took out this seed and asked me if I knew the name of the seed. I said that I didn't. She said that it's called the 'seed of peace' and if I looked closely at it, I would see that it's shaped just like a heart. She said the seed has a long history and I'd learn all about it as I went on my own journey. She said I should pay attention to everything that I saw along the way and notice how many things are shaped like the heart.

Then the old woman asked me to hold out my left hand, and she placed the seed in my palm. She then said that I should close my eyes, be present in my heart, and listen very carefully to what she was going to share. This is what she said:

"Peace is a seed planted
in the heart that grows
and blossoms from the
goodness of the heart.

Each day when you
wake up, no matter
how difficult it is,
open your eyes
with the feeling of
love in your heart.

Nurture this love as
you go through the day
with a kind deed for
someone in need,
a smile and kind words
for all those you meet.

Remember, an honest
day's work strengthens
the heart, and love
keeps the heart
tender and soft.

Remember to nurture your
heart with hope, faith,
beauty and love
until the seed of peace
blossoms in your heart, and
becomes the Flower of Peace
that you offer to the world.

Remember,
your words,

your deeds,
your work,
your glance,
even a smile
are the petals
of peace nurtured
each day from the
love in your heart.

Just imagine, if
everyone nurtured
their heart like this,
wouldn't the world
be a peaceful place to live?"

When the old woman finished speaking, she asked me to open my eyes and look at the seed in my palm. I had never seen anything like it; the seed had become pure light. The old woman said, "This seed of peace, that you take with you and offer to the world, will be the Flower of Peace that will adorn the world. Those who grow the seed of peace in their own hearts, just

148

like this seed, they, too, will be the light of peace in the world."

The angelic woman said that after the old woman gave her the message of the Flower of Peace, she told her that after she completed her mission, she should stay at that destination until a young man came along from a long journey of hardships. She was to care for him and when he was ready, she was to give him the gift of the Flower of Peace just as she had received it,

The angelic woman paused for a moment, looked deeply into my eyes and said, "You have now been trusted with the key to peace in the world. You have an important mission ahead. The Flower of Peace will flourish as you go from village to village, city to city, country to country. Keep hope, faith, and love in your heart as your trusted companions and you'll never feel alone nor discouraged.

At the end of your journey, you will arrive at a secret garden, the garden of love, and after sharing your story with the Goddess of Love, give her this seed for safekeeping. She already knows the one who will

LITTLE GARLIC

come along after you and who will take this message to the world."

Little Garlic and Onion talk about Adam's story

Onion paused for a moment, looked at Little Garlic, then said, "When Pumpkin and I heard the message of the Flower of Peace, we began to cry and cry. We knew we had been given a very special gift and were grateful for it. We didn't know why we were crying. We weren't sad. When we lifted our eyes, we saw Sweetheart looking at us tenderly. She understood what was going on inside of us.

"She said, 'Keep this story close to your heart and remember it every day as you go along your journey. The Flower of Peace will be your companion and friend along the way.'"

Onion paused, and quietly added, "I have never forgotten Sweetheart, and I've always remembered the story of Adam and the Flower of Peace."

"I'm sure I'll always remember these stories," said Little Garlic. "Onion, do you really think I will meet

150

Sweetheart someday, and she'll also give me a special gift?"

"I don't know," Onion answered. "She certainly didn't come to your dream for no reason. Besides, you must have been ready to hear this important story."

"Onion, did Adam tell Sweetheart about his travels?"

"Yes. He spent a long time with Sweetheart, and shared his experiences during his travels," replied Onion.

"Onion, will you share some of those stories with me?" asked Little Garlic. "I would really like to know where he went, what he learned, and what he discovered."

"I don't believe Sweetheart told us all the stories, but I'll share with you those that I remember as we travel along together," Onion replied.

"That would be wonderful! Thank you, Onion."

"You are most welcome!" Onion replied, then paused and said, in a quiet voice, "It's getting dark now. Let's get a good night's rest and recall the story of the Flower of Peace that Sweetheart shared.

Let it be our companion for the night."

"I like this idea very much. Thank you for sharing the story of Adam and the Flower of Peace. Sweetheart is in my heart, and I'll keep her close to my heart and remember her every day."

"I'm glad. I think the Flower of Peace was Sweetheart's gift to you. Good night, little fella. Rest well and sweet dreams."

"Good night, Onion. I'm so grateful, peaceful, and happy. Thank you for being my friend."

Onion glanced tenderly at his young friend. This was the first time he had shared the story of Sweetheart with anyone. He wondered if Secret Star had a special mission in mind for Little Garlic. Indeed, these were special days.

Little Garlic will be back with more stories
as his journey continues!

The Author

 THIS book reflects Avideh Shashaani's unique international experience as a poet, writer, and lecturer, and her life's work as a passionate, unyielding advocate for children, and supporter of youth projects for interreligious understanding, peace, and social justice.

Shashaani is the sixth annual recipient of the "Waging Peace" award instituted by former president Jimmy Carter.

She is the founder and president of the Fund for the Future of our Children (FFC), which for almost three decades has nurtured young people as tomorrow's leaders for peace and social justice. FFC has drawn attention to the plight of children in war-torn countries and developed curriculum on moral leadership called "Speaking Truth: Watershed Moments in Global Leadership."

Shashaani's poetry and writings on spirituality and advocacy for children have featured in a one-hour program in the Library of Congress radio series for National Public Radio stations. She is the author of three books of poetry. *Tell Me Where to Be Born* focuses on violence against children. Her poetry and writings have appeared in anthologies, books and journals including *Spirituality in Clinical Practice of the American Psychological Association*. She is the editor of *Something Deeper Happened: Young Voices and the 2008 U.S. Election* with a foreword by Archbishop Desmond Tutu.

Avideh Shashaani has served on various nonprofit boards involved with spirituality, including the Faith and Politics Institute that sponsors Congressional pilgrimages, Thomas Merton Institute for Contemplative Living, and the Collaborative for Spirituality in Education.

She has been a guest speaker at many prestigious institutions, ranging from the Parliament of World Religions, United Nations Conference on Human Rights, to Columbia University, Georgetown University, Washington Hebrew Congregation, the Goethe Institute, and the Cincinnati Museum of Art.

Her work has included bringing meditation and wellness programs to corporations, organizations and government agencies including the U.S. Senate, U.S. Capitol Police, World Bank, Pan American Health Organization, American Heart Association, MCI, and INTELSAT.

Early in her career, Shashaani was the first co-director of the International Institute for Rehabilitation in Developing Countries founded by the United Nations and was appointed by the UN Secretary General to the United Nations Expert Group Meeting on the "Socio-Economic Implication of Investments in Rehabilitation of the Disabled."

Born in Tehran, Iran, Shashaani spent much of her childhood in Washington, D. C. where her father was a diplomat. Her academic training includes a B.A. in experimental psychology, an M.A. in educational planning and management, and a Ph.D. in Sufi Studies.

Visit **www.LittleGarlic.org**

Acknowledgments

Thank you to all who have supported *Little Garlic* on this journey to publication.